Smokey Charlotte Midnight Tommy Casper

Rusty Blanche Sebastian Toodles Luigi

Sweet Pea Alfalfa Gladys Bon Ton Toby

I LIKE CATS

By Patricia Hubbell · Illustrated by Pamela Paparone

A Cheshire Studio Book · North-South Books · New York · London

Cha-Cha Lord Buttons Marc Romeo Popcorn

Miau-Miau OTTO Catalina Moritz Nacho Grande

Mouse Wishbone Tinker Bell Pickles Jones Nacho

To Shoshi, with love —P.H.
To Marc —P.P.

A CHESHIRE STUDIO BOOK
Published in the United States by North-South Books Inc., New York.
Published simultaneously in Great Britain, Canada, Australia, and New Zealand in 2003
by North-South Books, an imprint of Nord-Süd Verlag AG, Gossau Zürich, Switzerland.
Library of Congress Cataloging-in-Publication Data is available. A CIP catalogue record
for this book is available from The British Library.
ISBN 0-7358-1774-X (trade edition) 10 9 8 7 6 5 4 3 2 1
ISBN 0-7358-1775-8 (library edition) 10 9 8 7 6 5 4 3 2 1
Printed in Hong Kong
Visit our web site: www.northsouth.com

I like cats.

Thin cats, fat cats,

curl-up-in-my-hat cats.

sneak-a-little-snack cats.

Grey cats,
brown cats,

parade-around-the-town cats.

Cats with stripes,

cats with socks,

cats with orange polka dots.

Cats in baskets,

boxes,

vases,

cats in
all their hiding
places.

Cats that pounce

or curl in nooks,

china cats
and cats in books.

Cats that wrestle
gloves and mittens,

cats alone

or cats with kittens.

Farm cats,

city cats,

sing-a-little-ditty cats.

Fluffy cats, sleek cats,

kiss-me-on-the-cheek cats.

Prowling cats, howling cats,
wake-me-with-their-yowling cats.

Cats on tables,

cats on chairs,

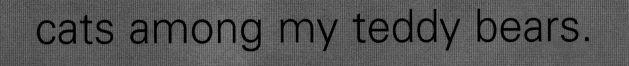

cats among my teddy bears.

on my tummy,
on my head,
on my toes
and in my bed.

I like cats,
it's plain to see.
I like cats—

and CATS LIKE ME!